Swimmy

This Book Belongs To:

_____

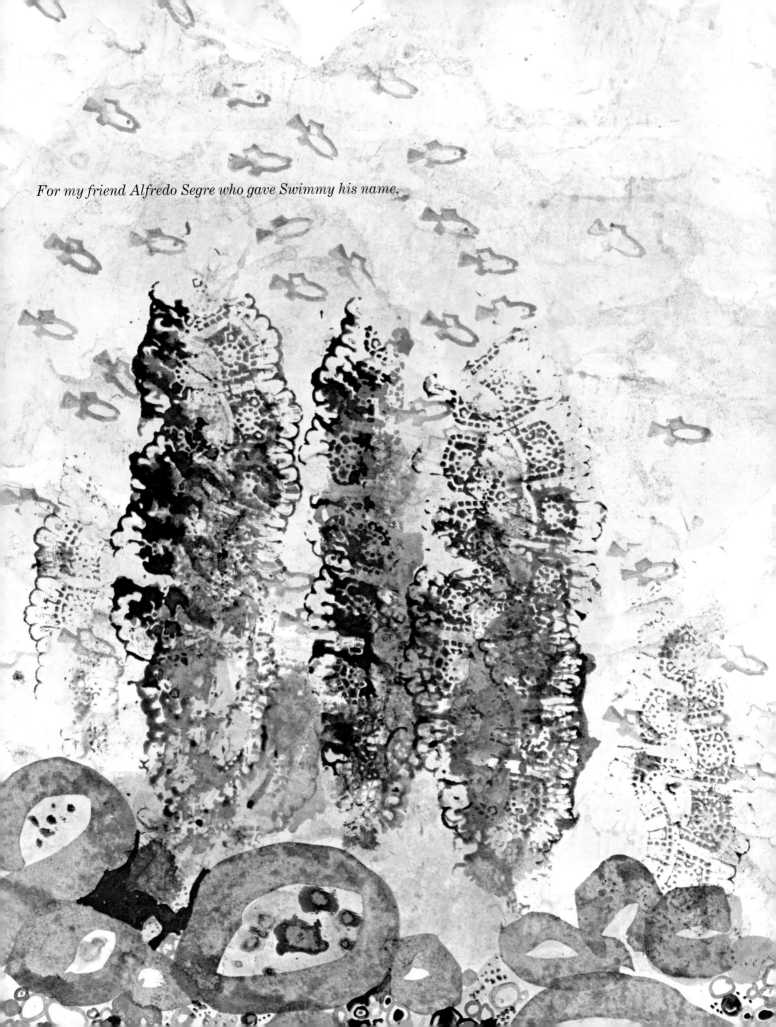

For my friend Alfredo Segre who gave Swimmy his name.

Swimmy

by Leo Lionni

Dragonfly Books —➤ *New York*

A happy school of little fish lived in a corner of the sea somewhere.
They were all red. Only one of them was as black as a mussel shell.
He swam faster than his brothers and sisters. His name was Swimmy.

One bad day a tuna fish, swift, fierce and very hungry, came darting through the waves. In one gulp he swallowed all the little red fish. Only Swimmy escaped.

He swam away in the deep wet world. He was scared, lonely and very sad.

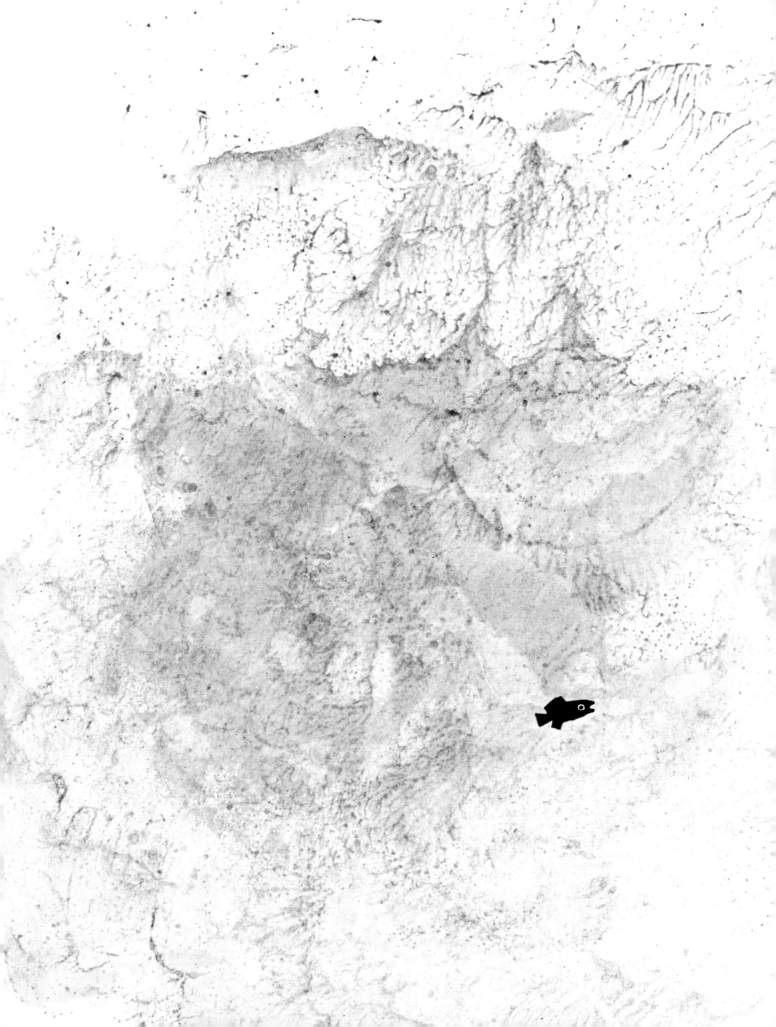

But the sea was full of wonderful creatures, and as he swam from marvel to marvel Swimmy was happy again.

He saw a medusa made of rainbow jelly . . .

a lobster, who walked about like a water-moving machine . . .

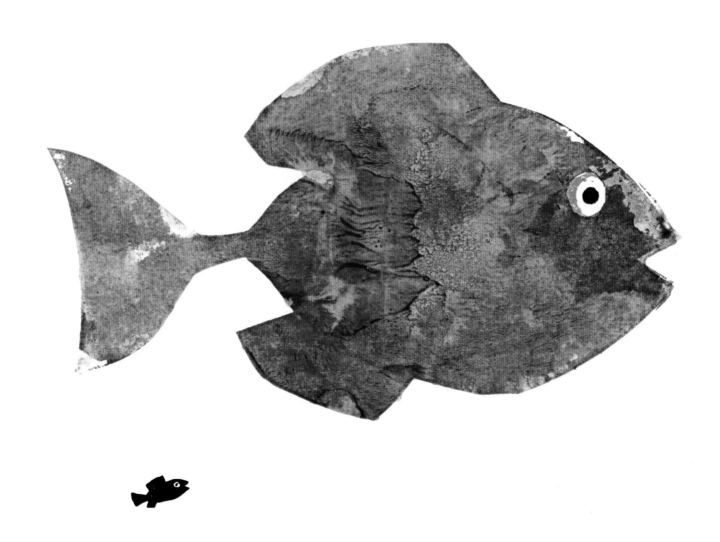

strange fish, pulled by an invisible thread . . .

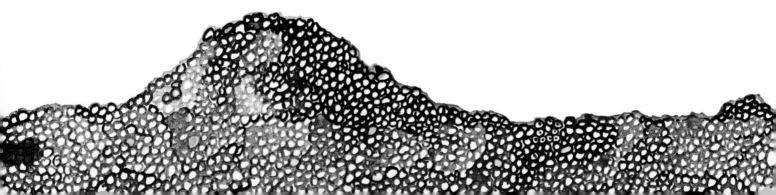

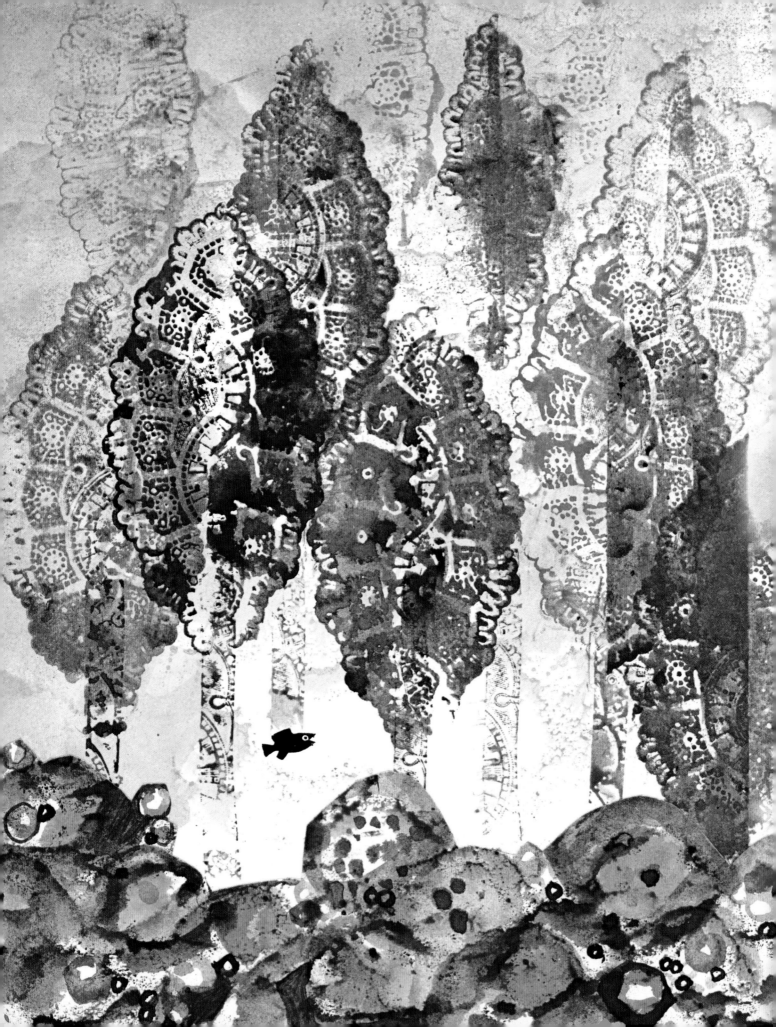

a forest of seaweeds growing from sugar-candy rocks . . .

an eel whose tail was almost too far away to remember . . .

and sea anemones, who looked like pink palm trees swaying in the wind.

Then, hidden in the dark shade of rocks and weeds, he saw a school of little fish, just like his own.

"Let's go and swim and play and SEE things!" he said happily.
"We can't," said the little red fish. "The big fish will eat us all."

"But you can't just lie there," said Swimmy. "We must THINK of something."

Swimmy thought and thought and thought.

Then suddenly he said, "I have it!"
"We are going to swim all together like the biggest fish in the sea!"

He taught them to swim close together, each in his own place,

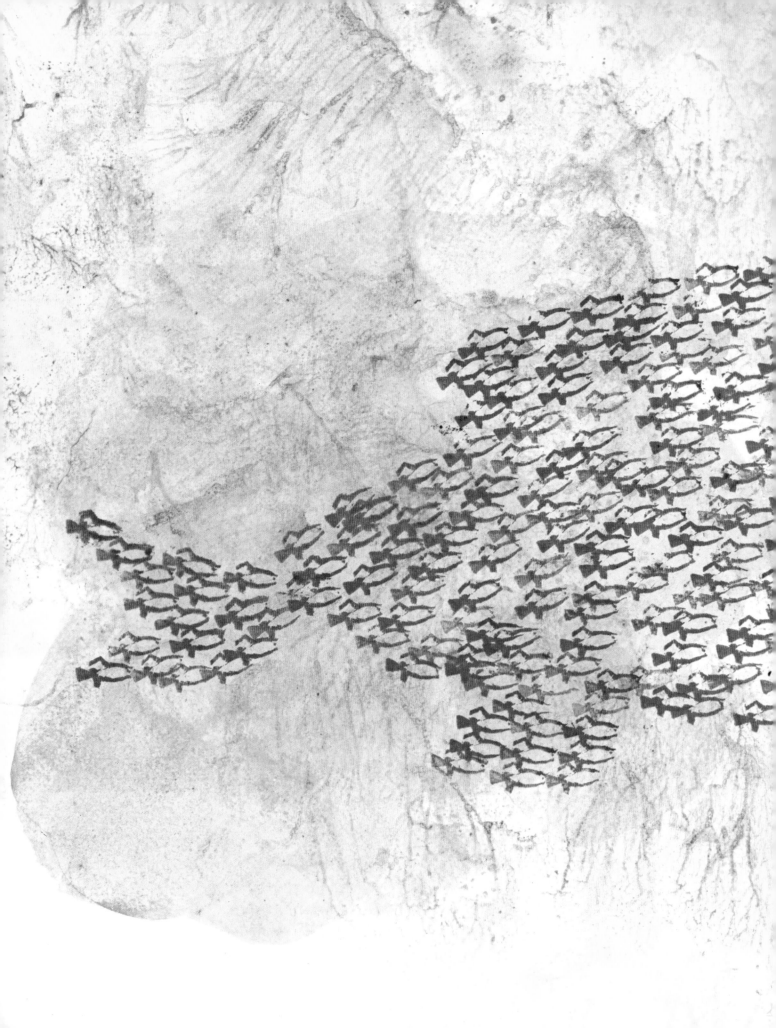

and when they had learned to swim like one giant fish, he said, "I'll be the eye."

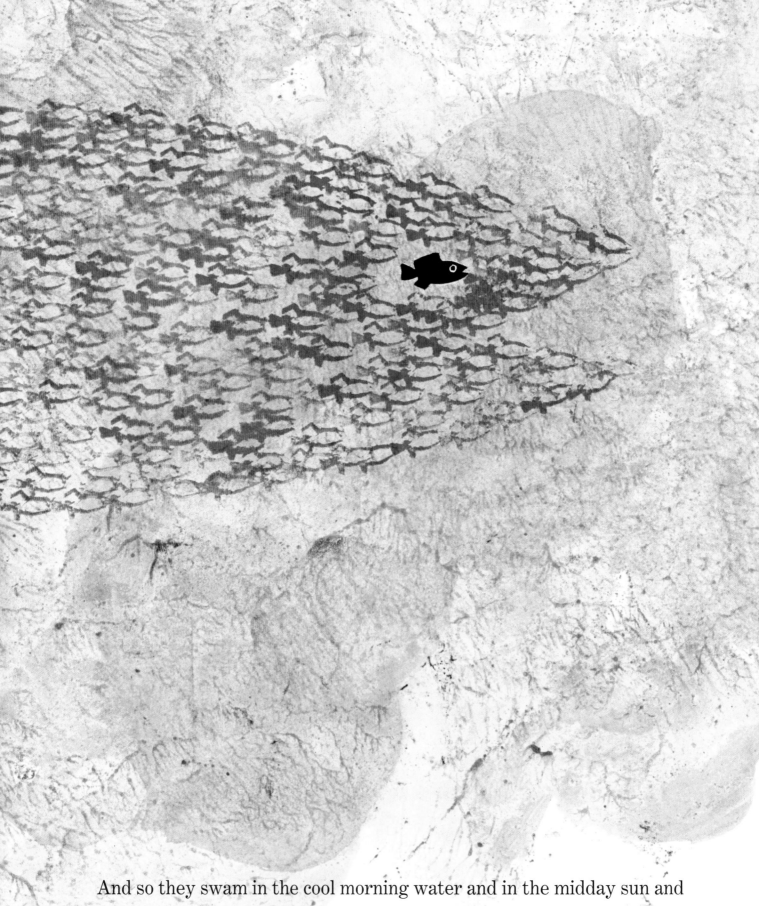

And so they swam in the cool morning water and in the midday sun and

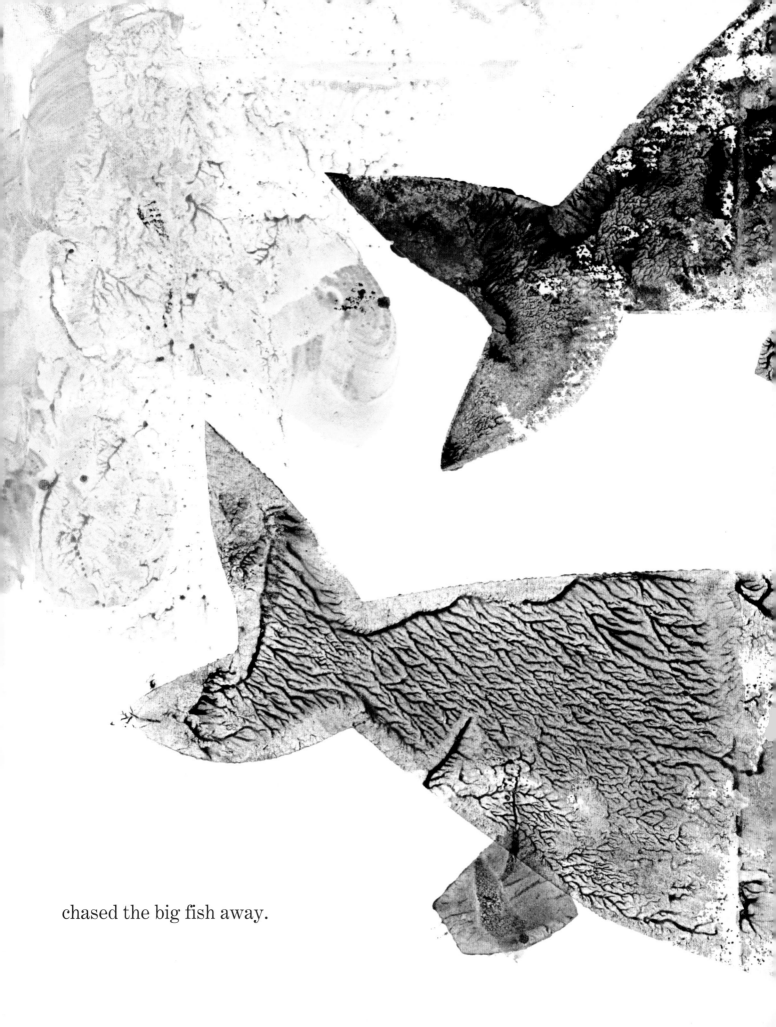

chased the big fish away.

All rights reserved. Published in the United States by Dragonfly Books, an imprint of Random House Children's Books, a division of Penguin Random House LLC, New York. Originally published in hardcover in the United States by Pantheon Books, New York, in 1963.

Dragonfly Books with the colophon is a registered trademark of Penguin Random House LLC.

Visit us on the Web! randomhousekids.com

Educators and librarians, for a variety of teaching tools, visit us at RHTeachersLibrarians.com

The Library of Congress has cataloged the hardcover edition of this work as follows:
Lionni, Leo.
Swimmy / by Leo Lionni.
p.   cm.
Summary: A little black fish in a school of red fish figures out a way of protecting them all from their natural enemies.
ISBN 978-0-394-81713-2 (trade) — ISBN 978-0-394-91713-9 (lib. bdg)
[1. Fishes—Fiction.]
I. Title
PZ10.3.L6465 Sw
63008504
ISBN 978-0-399-55550-3 (pbk.)

MANUFACTURED IN CHINA
January 2017
11